TASSO

by Papas.

Pikku Publishing

This edition published in the United Kingdom in 2017 by Pikku Publishing, 7 High Street, Barkway, Hertfordshire, SG8 8EA
www.pikkupublishing.com

ISBN: 978-0-9934884-4-3

Copyright in this edition © 2017 Pikku Publishing

First published in the United Kingdom in 1966 by Oxford University Press.

Copyright in text and illustrations © Theresa J Papas

1 3 5 7 9 10 8 6 4 2

Printed in China by Toppan Leefung Printing Ltd.

Tasso and Athena lived in a seaside village in Greece. They had no mother, and their father was a fisherman. Like most fishermen, he was poor.

So, to help their father, Tasso and Athena worked in a café, called the Trocadero. They worked there during their long summer holiday and at the weekends as well.

Athena served the people with food, and Tasso played his bouzouki.

He was a wonderful player, and the villagers and tourists loved to sing and dance to his music. Even the donkeys brayed happily — though not in tune! — and the goats jumped and skipped with joy.

But there was one difficulty. After playing tune after tune for several hours, Tasso had to stop for a rest.

The villagers and tourists begged him to go on playing, but Tasso was just too tired.

The disappointed people drifted away, and the owner of the café wrung his hands in despair. He knew that Tasso could not help being tired, but, 'If only,' he said, 'I could find something that would go on playing without stopping, my café would be full day and night.'

Then he heard of the Rock-a-Rola machine, and decided to buy one.

One morning, when Tasso and Athena arrived at the Trocadero
there it stood – the Rock-a-Rola! 'Press the button!' cried the
proprietor excitedly.

Athena pressed it gingerly, and immediately lights flashed, bells buzzed and music blared forth.

All the people came running, and stared in amazement at the new machine.

It went on playing and playing all day long without a pause. The proprietor was pleased, and told Tasso that he would not be wanted any more because the Trocadero had all the music it needed.

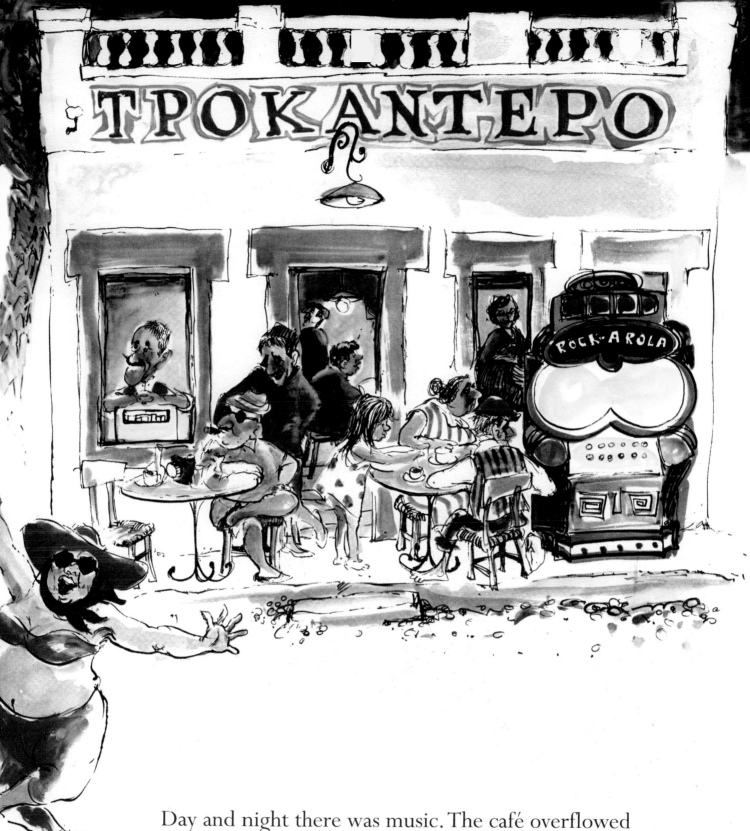

Day and night there was music. The café overflowed with customers and Athena worked hard. The proprietor was happy.

But Tasso was very sad. He put away his bouzouki and helped his father with the fishing.

After a while, the customers grew tired of so much music. They could hardly hear themselves speak, and could not enjoy their usual chat about the weather or the fishing or the crops. So they stayed away from the Trocadero.

The proprietor noticed
this, and turned the volume
of the Rock-a-Rola louder to
attract more customers. But
the louder he turned it up, the
more the people stayed away,
and the more they stayed away,
the louder he turned it up.

The noise could be heard all
over the village, and no one could
get to sleep because of it.

At last the villagers went to complain to the Chief of Police, who passed a law saying that the Rock-a-Rola must not be played after nine o'clock at night.

Then the proprietor started playing it earlier in the morning, so another law had to be passed saying that the Rock-a-Rola must not be played before nine o'clock in the morning.

Then other laws were passed about the volume and the kind of music that could be played, and slowly the village became quiet and sad and dull. Nobody went to the Trocadero, nobody sang or danced, the donkeys became impossible and the goats just sat.

Athena had to leave the Trocadero because there was no work for her to do. She went home very sad, and while looking for a handkerchief to dry her eyes she found Tasso's bouzouki.

'Play something, Tasso.' she said. 'It is the only thing that will make me happy again.'

So Tasso played. The people down the street heard and came out to listen. They gathered round Tasso and began to sing and dance.

The proprietor came, too, and they carried Tasso on their shoulders back to the Trocadero.

Then they carried
the Rock-a-Rola on
their shoulders, and put
it in a boat and sailed
out into deep water.
There they dropped the
Rock-a-Rola overboard,
and it sank to the
bottom of the sea.

The people came back to the café, and the proprietor cooked a special feast and invited everyone to be his guest.

And all the people ate and drank, and danced and sang and were very, very happy – especially Tasso and Athena.